Rosie's Fishing Trip

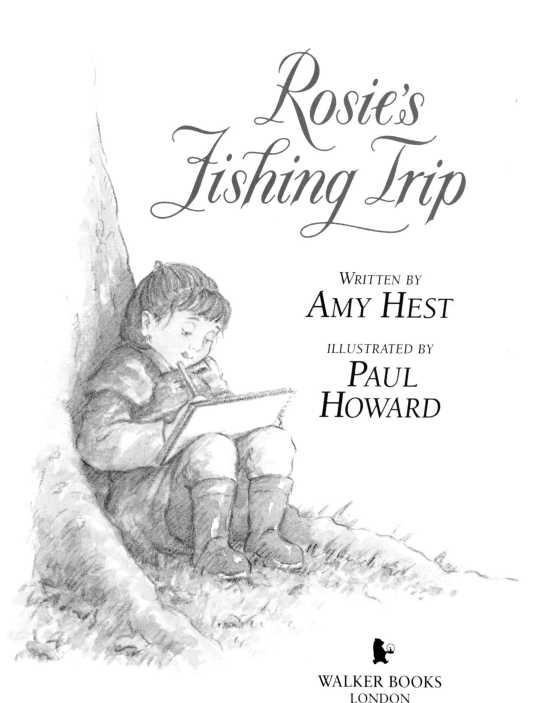

WRITTEN BY
AMY HEST

ILLUSTRATED BY
PAUL HOWARD

WALKER BOOKS
LONDON

Rosie's bicycle had two fat tyres and a saddlebag at the back. There was a wide wicker basket at the front, and it was filling up fast with everything Rosie needed for her fishing trip, including three rolls and an old red Thermos flask with chocolate milk inside.

Rosie wrapped her silver spoon in a cherry-coloured napkin. She wrapped her tiny jar of jam in yellow tissue paper. She taped two pink pencils to her special drawing pad to make a picture, later, that would hang on someone's wall.

"Time to go fishing!" called Rosie.

"Good luck, my love!" Mum came to the kitchen to see her off. Her dressing-gown was soft and green and smelt of talcum powder. (At night Mum liked curling up in her dressing-gown in her big chair near the window. Sometimes Rosie curled up too, and they took turns reading in a soft, night voice.)

Rosie's fishing coat had a cape across the back and seven slender buckles that buckled up the front.

Mum kissed both her cheeks.

Then Rosie bumped her bicycle down
the steps all the way to Front Street,
where it was still dark. Rosie shivered.
She did not like the dark much.

But she did like fishing and of course
Granpa, who was waiting on a corner
near the park.

Rosie sucked in. She let her breath out.

Pedal, Rosie, pedal! There were too many shadows in the village in the morning. It was chilly and there was mist in the air, or maybe it was drizzle. *Pedal, Rosie, pedal!*

In between big houses and others
that were small, the sun was trying to
light up the village. *I am racing you, sun,
and I will win the race to Granpa!* Rosie
pedalled hard and she pedalled very
fast, stopping at every crossing.

Granpa was waiting. Rosie rode and
he walked along with his big fishing
bucket and his tall fishing rod. They
rode and walked all the way to
Periwinkle Pond.

Rosie leaned her bicycle against a
tree. Granpa draped a cloth on a grassy
spot nearby. They each ate a roll with
strawberry jam. Then they shared another.

"Tell me a poem, Granpa, and please
make it rhyme," said Rosie.

Granpa shook the Thermos to make
a million chocolate bubbles that popped
on Rosie's nose.

"A poem about me is a good idea."

Sometimes Granpa made up a poem that spilled right out. Other times they had to wait. Sometimes Granpa scratched words on paper. Other times he plucked words from the air.

While they waited for a poem, they went down to the lake and into the water way past their ankles. Granpa's fishing boots came up to his knees. Rosie's fishing boots used to be her mother's. They were still too big for her, but she loved them anyway.

Granpa held the rod over the lake. They waited for fish. Rosie held the rod too, but it was heavy, and still no fish. *Come-on-fish-come-on!*

When Rosie's legs were tired, she leaned
against a tree and drew a beautiful picture
of Granpa fishing in the lake in the mist

in the morning. She sketched a dog, too.
Rosie liked drawing dogs. And Granpa
liked hanging the pictures on his wall.

After a long, long time Granpa's fishing rod curved. Then it bounced. Rosie's heart bounced too. *Fish beware!* She reeled in the line. *You feel big, fish, but Rosie is strong!* She jiggled the line. *I'm going to get you, fish, and bring you home to Mum to cook for lunch!* Rosie reeled that fish right out of the lake.

The fish looked at Rosie and
Rosie looked back. He was small,
like a fist, and wriggly and scared.

They tossed him back and he swam
away with his cousins.

So-long-fish-so-long!

Rosie and Granpa rode and walked
through the village. There wasn't a
single fish in the bucket, but they
didn't mind. Granpa was thinking up
a poem, and Rosie was helping with
the rhymes. The sun came out and
the sky cleared up, and Mum kissed
them on both cheeks.

Lunch was waiting. They each had
a bowl of pasta. Afterwards there
was ice-cream with hundreds
and thousands. And after
that, Granpa recited
their poem:

Rosie's Fishing Trip

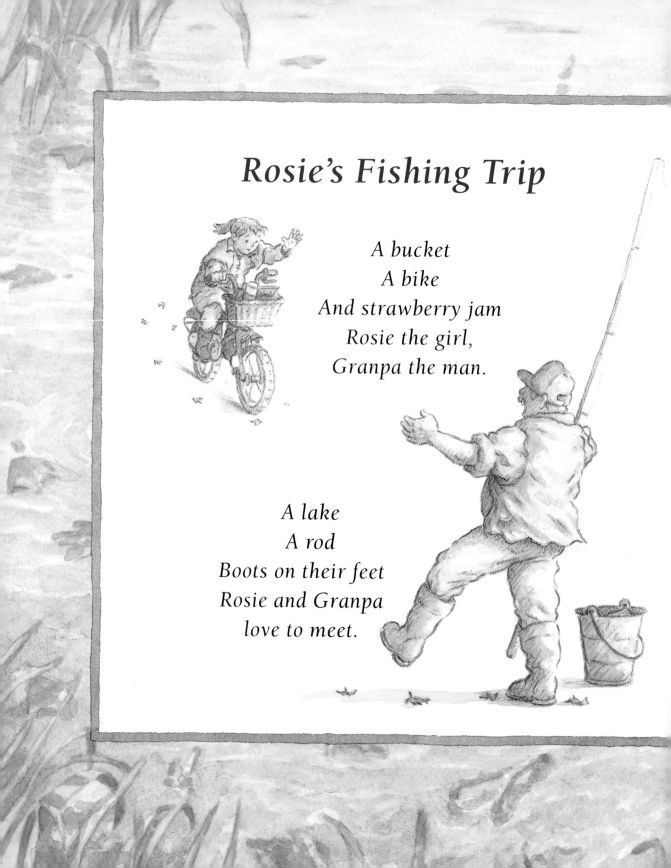

A bucket
A bike
And strawberry jam
Rosie the girl,
Granpa the man.

A lake
A rod
Boots on their feet
Rosie and Granpa
love to meet.

A snack
A chat
Then fishing time
Come-on-fish,
nibble this line!

A pull
A tug
Sweet baby fish!
How dare we put
you in a dish?

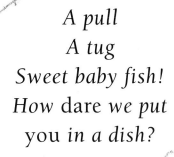

A splish
A splash
So-long, swim away
Sweet baby fish,
it's your lucky day!